In memory of the Columbia 7

POCKET
BOOKS

First published in Great Britain in 2004 by Pocket Books,
an imprint of Simon & Schuster UK Ltd,
Africa House, 64-78 Kingsway, London WC2B 6AH

Originally published in the USA in 2004 by Atheneum Books for Young Readers,
an imprint of Simon & Schuster Children's Publishing Division, New York

A CIP catalogue record for this book is available from the British Library upon request

Book design by Ann Bobco
The text for this book was set in Granjon
The illustrations are rendered in watercolour, coloured pencils and litho pencils

ISBN 0743478800

Manufactured in China

1 3 5 7 9 10 8 6 4 2

RAÚL COLÓN

ORSON BLASTS OFF!

POCKET BOOKS

London   New York   Sydney

"Oh, no!!!"

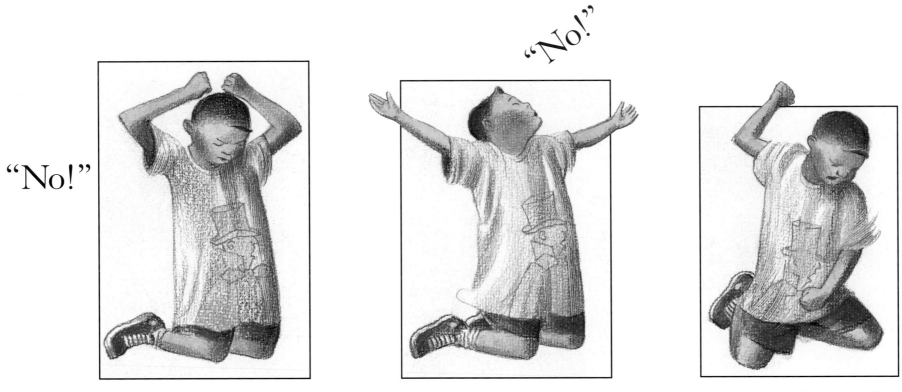

"You stupid computer, how could you? Now there's no way I can play
Arctic Adventure, or Whale Storm, or Starship Boomerang, or anything."

"Rats! I think I'm bored already!"

"Ahem! Orson? Excuse me, sir. No need to get upset."

"Who's that?"

"It is I, Weasel.
May I kindly ask you to step outside?"

"Outside? I don't *do* outside. Anyway, all that's there is a pile of stupid snow. Hey, wait a minute – snow? In July? And . . . you can talk?"

"There certainly is, sir. And I certainly can."

"Yahoo, snow in July! Now, let's see. I'll need my coat and gloves, these old tennis rackets, some very thick rope, my backpack, and . . ."

"Orson, sir, I kindly beg you to need *me*."

"Okay, okay. . . . And I'll need you too, Weasel."

"And that must be a southerly breeze – or are you breathing down my neck?"

"Respectfully, sir, it is not I, and it is not a breeze . . . unless a breeze is white and round with big, dark eyes and giant paws."

"Sir, I think we're trapped. The water looks remarkably chilly, and I believe I see a storm approaching."

"Don't worry, Weasel. I have an idea that should get us out of here."

"You know, some storms have eyes, Weasel. And if this one does, and it can see us, maybe it won't hurt us."

"Maybe, sir. Why, there's an eye!"

"Y-e-e-e-s-s-s-s! We're saved."

"Captain Orson, the boat is about to sink. I suggest you hold on to your hat."

"Am I glad to be back on dry land! Just look at those stars, Weasel."

"They're twinkling at us, sir."

"Which gives me another idea . . ."

"Sir, please. You can't possibly think your idea will fly."

"Of course it will. Give me a hand and start the countdown."

"Ten . . . *this is madness* . . . seven, six, five . . . *madness, I say* . . . two, one . . ."

"Blast off, sir."

"We did it, Weasel!
We're in orbit!
This is *so* cool!"

"Just look at those stars and those planets and those comets and those meteors and those moons! Isn't that the Big Dipper? I love it!"

"I'm glad someone does, sir."

"I think I can see a black hole ahead. Let's get closer."

"Why would we want to do that, sir?"

"Why *wouldn't* we want to?"

"Orson, sir, it appears
we're falling!
Falling down!
Falling up!
Falling sideways!"

TICK TOCK. TICK TOCK. TICK TOCK.

"Hey, Weasel, we're home. Wasn't that an amazing adventure?

Hey, Weasel, are you asleep? Oh well, I guess I'll go and play . . .

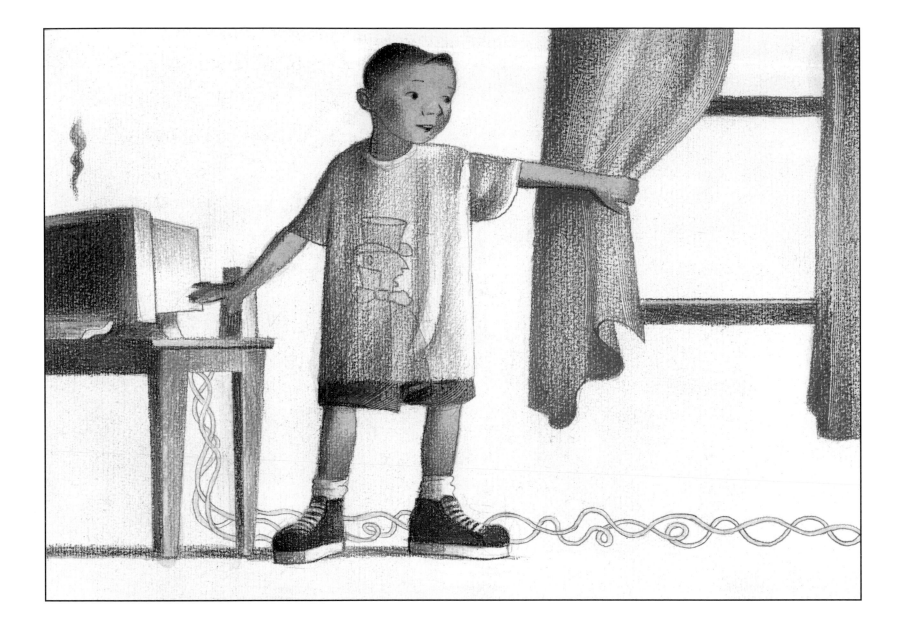

. . . outside."

A Note About the Text

Orson Blasts Off! plays with scientific terms and idiomatic expressions — phrases that do not mean what they appear to mean. Some are, in order of appearance:

North Pole: This is not a pole in the ground, but the final destination for travellers who follow their compass needle north from anywhere on Earth.

eye of the storm: At the centre of a cyclone or hurricane, all is calm, as winds, rain, and thunder rage around it. There is little or no cloud cover here. This is called the "eye" of the storm, although there is no real eye.

whale of a tale: This phrase — not necessarily about our largest mammal — can mean any very exaggerated or impressive story.

Big Dipper: Part of the constellation Ursa Major, it was given its name because its seven bright stars form the shape of a bowl and handle.

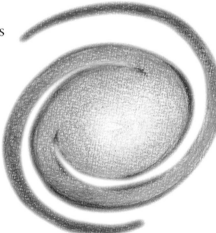

black hole: This is an astronomical term referring to a region of space where mass is so great that nothing — not even light — can escape its gravitational pull.